In Our Mothers' House

In Our Mothers' House

Patricia Polacco

PHILOMEL
BOOKS

When my mothers told me about how they brought me home to live with them shortly after I was born, their eyes would shine and glisten and they'd grin from ear to ear.

They told me how they had walked across dry hot deserts, sailed through turbulent seas, flew over tall mountains and trekked through fierce storms just to bring me home.

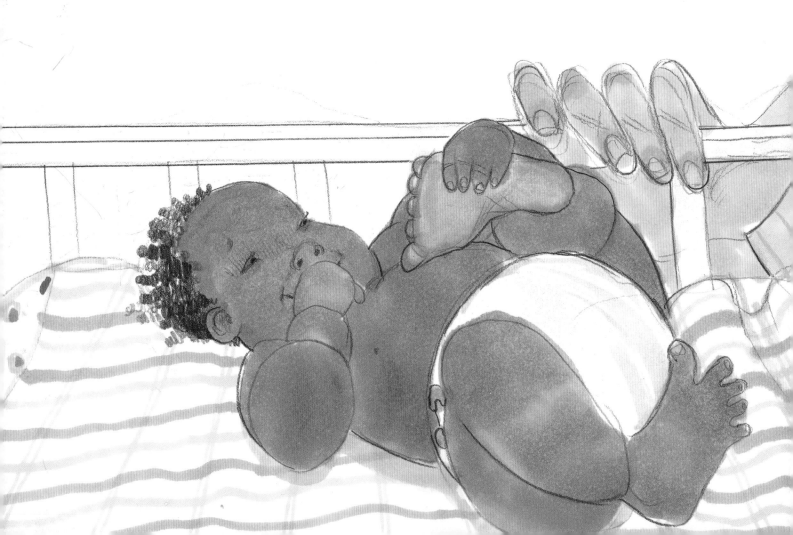

Then they'd both get tears in their eyes when they'd tell me what it was like to hold me in their arms for the very first time.

Three years after I was born, my brother Will came to us. He was so tiny, just three days old.

Then there was Millie. We always kidded that our mothers found her under a lily pad in an enchanted pond deep in a hidden forest. She became part of our family when she was two months old, three years after Will had come.

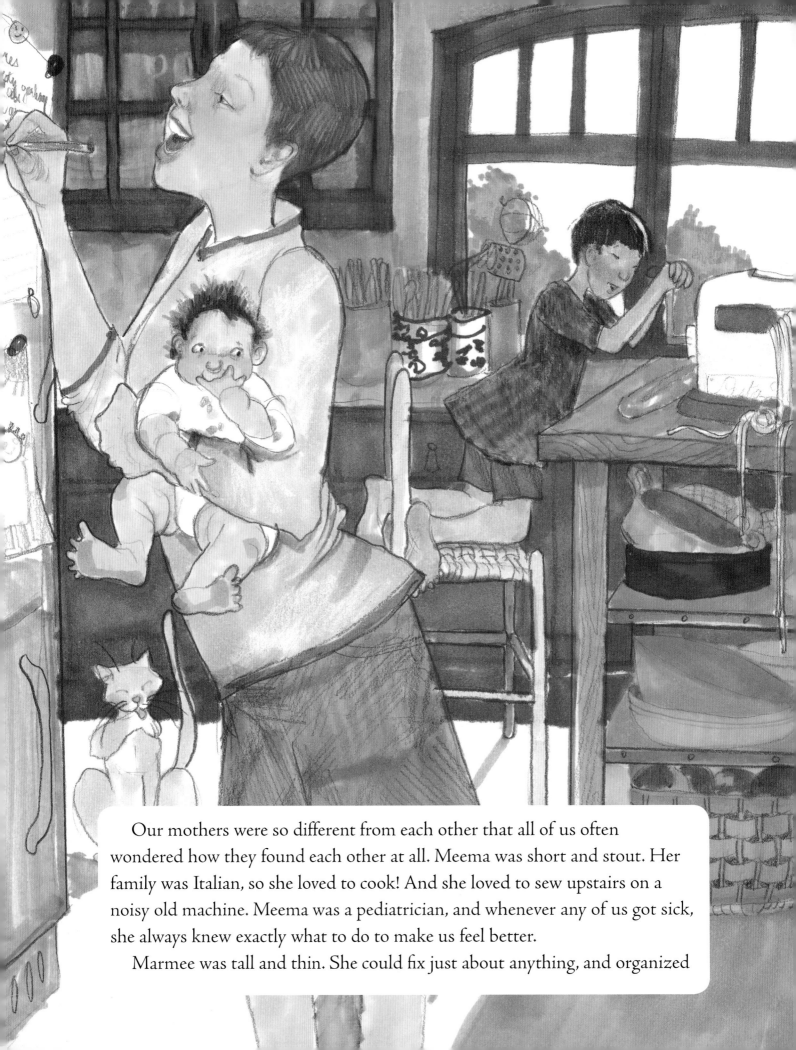

Our mothers were so different from each other that all of us often wondered how they found each other at all. Meema was short and stout. Her family was Italian, so she loved to cook! And she loved to sew upstairs on a noisy old machine. Meema was a pediatrician, and whenever any of us got sick, she always knew exactly what to do to make us feel better.

Marmee was tall and thin. She could fix just about anything, and organized

everything. She made lists, posted chores on the refrigerator and kept the house so clean and tidy. We used to kid her that if we got up in the middle of the night to go to the bathroom, she'd make our beds before we could climb back into them!

Marmee was a paramedic who rode in an ambulance. Whenever there was any kind of emergency, she always remained calm and took charge.

Our mothers loved to laugh. Meema's whole body shook when she laughed. Marmee laughed almost silently, but she'd laugh so hard that she'd practically fall down and go limp.

Our mothers' house was always alive with music. All kinds! Sometimes our mothers would put on old rock-and-roll or swing records and get all of us to dance with them.

"This is the Hully Gully," Meema would sing out. Once she flapped her arms like wings and clucked. "The Chicken Dance."

"And this is bebop," Marmee said as she grabbed Will and spun him around, then dipped him backward. We laughed and laughed.

We lived in a big old brown shingle house on Woolsey Street in Berkeley, California, that was set back from the street. When we walked into our mothers' house, the first thing we saw was the staircase. All of us slid down the banisters. Once, Will was sliding so fast that he couldn't stop at the bottom. He flew off and took the finial with him.

In the living room, the old clinker brick fireplace was the heart of our home. Sometimes Marmee and Meema'd pop corn in it, and we'd all sit, eat popcorn and apples and share stories.

It was Millie's favorite place to be. I remember when she was about two, she got up in the middle of the night. We found her the next morning asleep

in the hearth, covered with charcoal. She had taken a piece of charcoal and drawn all over the nearby wall.

We couldn't take our eyes off her drawing—it was so beautiful. If we hadn't known it before, we knew then just how magical Millie was. "Well, my little sparrow," Meema finally whispered, "looks like you are a magnificent artist."

The most favored place to be for us kids was the sunroom above the carport. That is where all of our toys lived. It was where we played dress-up and where every Halloween costume we wore began. No store-bought costumes for us! Marmee and Millie designed them, and Meema would help us sew them.

One year we went as wild animals. Hardly any of our neighbors recognized us. That is, except for Mrs. Lockner. She knew us all right. She glared at us when she opened the door. She glared at our mothers, too. Her kids came running and were really excited to see us, but Mrs. Lockner turned her back and shut the door.

"What's the matter with her?" Will blurted out. But our mothers said nothing and continued down the block.

Even so, it was one of the best Halloweens we ever had. We even won the Claremont Avenue costume contest that year!

Our upstairs bathroom was almost big enough to hold our entire family at one time. It almost did, too. I remember the night that all of us kids came down with the flu. All at once! Meema and Marmee were darting between each of our rooms. Will, Millie and I were throwing up. Our mothers changed sheets, washed pajamas and bathed our foreheads with a cool washcloth. I loved how soft their hands were when they touched my face and wiped away my tears.

After two days of utter misery our mothers announced that they had a surprise for us. "This should make you feel better," Marmee sang out.

We opened our eyes and there they stood, holding two adorable puppies.

When those puppies started jumping about and licking our faces, we all squealed with joy. We finally named them Miso and Wasabi.

One of the best things about our mothers' house was the tree house that
we built in the backyard. Practically the entire neighborhood helped us. It
all started with Will, who, like Marmee, was always building things. One
Saturday he found some plans for a tree house in a magazine and went to her.

It took several weekends to finish, but the Saturday that we did finish it,
everyone stood in a circle around the tree house. Marmee and Meema broke a
bottle of soda over the doorjamb and named the tree house Thistle House!

That night, all of us kids got to sleep there. Even the Lockner kids were invited, but their parents came and got them. They barely spoke to us—just pulled them down the driveway. They just plain didn't like us, I guessed. I couldn't quite understand why. We always tried to be respectful and friendly, the way our mothers taught us to be.

The kitchen in our mothers' house was the center of everything that was happening in our household. The kitchen doorway was where us kids got measured each year. Meema and Marmee's handwriting is still there even now.

And all of our family holidays began in the kitchen. Our grandparents, aunts, uncles and cousins usually came for the weekend. Our Italian grampa, our *nonno*, was in charge of cooking. We all loved gnocchi!

We'd all help him unload the perfect Roma tomatoes, the oxtails, the pork shanks and the beef brisket. We peeled onions, shaved and diced carrots and chopped fresh herbs from the garden.

After the sauce had been cooking for most of the day, all of us stood at the kitchen island. Nonno made a well in the middle of a hill of flour and broke several eggs into it. Then he riced very hot boiled potatoes right into

the flour well. He'd shake his hands from the heat of it as he kneaded the
volcano of flour, eggs and potatoes into a dough.

   Then Marmee and Meema rolled the dough into long tubes. Millie and Will
got to cut them into small pillows. Then I ran each pillow over the back of a
floured fork. Nonno dropped the gnocchi into boiling water.

   When they floated to the top, they were done. Sauce and potato dumplings
were dished up, salads were made and baguettes of French bread from the
bakery were carried to the table, where we were all so ready to eat.

At our table we didn't only eat, though. Marmee and Meema made sure of that. Everyone talked about everything. Politics, sports, music and art. Their voices got louder and louder. Opera was always playing in the background. Then they'd all burst into laughter that shook the table. Nonno would pound his fist and laugh the loudest. What I loved the most about our family was that we could all speak our hearts. We never measured words.

After dinner, all of us kids would sit on the stairs with our grandparents. This is when they'd tell us about when they were young in the old country. It was the best part of the day. Marmee and Meema would listen in and smile.

One of the niftiest things that happened in our neighborhood was the Woolsey Street block party. Marmee organized it. It became a tradition.

For that first one, Millie and I made all of the invitations by hand, and Meema took us around to deliver them from door to door. Everyone was invited. When we stopped at the Lockners' house, their mother glared at us, the way she always did.

"Why doesn't that lady like us, Meema?" I asked my mother.

She just smiled at me and hugged me up. "I like you, baby," she said, and we went on our way.

The day of our big block party arrived! Each of the houses on the street had to invent some sort of game in their front yard. The McGuires across the street had a land-mine contest. A blindfolded player had to pick his way past marshmallow "mines" while a caller warned him where they were.

The Goldsteins had a penny toss on saucers. The Brooks family had a dunk tank. A lot of fathers got dunked that day. The Abdullas had a fishing booth.

I think our family had the best game of all—a miniature golf course. Will, Marmee and I put it together. We lashed together old rain gutters with traps and obstacles that had to be putted around in order to get to the end: a flowerpot buried to the top. It was Marmee's great idea.

"Aren't we all something," Meema said when she saw our food court. On our street everyone was so different, that's what Meema meant. So the Mardicians brought stuffed grape leaves and ground lamb. The Polos brought spanakopita and Greek salads. The Abdullas brought hummus and tabouli.

Nonno made a huge pot of spaghetti and fried schnitzel. The Yamagakis brought sushi, which I liked a lot. But Meema passed it up for fried clams and crawdads and corn on the cob, which the Barbers had made.

At the end of the day, when everyone was cleaning up and getting ready to sit in our backyard and just talk, Meema looked up to see Mrs. Lockner coming down the street. The Lockners had been invited but hadn't come. She planted her feet squarely in front of our mothers.

"I don't appreciate what you two are!" she snarled at Meema and Marmee.

Will and Millie came running up. I froze where I was. Mrs. Lockner wheeled and stalked off.

"What's the matter with her, Momma, what's the matter with her?" Millie kept saying.

All the neighbors closed in on us.

"She is full of fear, sweetie. She's afraid of what she cannot understand: she doesn't understand *us*," Meema quietly said.

"There seems to be no love in her heart, either," whispered Marmee.

The neighbors agreed—the Mardicians, the Polos, the Yamagakis, the Kiernans, the Goldsteins, the Abdullas, everybody—and one by one they hugged our mothers. Then, they all stayed and talked and talked until late that night, thanking Meema more than once for thinking up the block party.

There wasn't a day in my life that I didn't feel deeply loved and wanted by Meema and Marmee. Our mothers were willing to do anything for us. We knew that.

Here's what I mean. One day Millie and I ran all the way home from school and came tumbling into the kitchen with news.

"Meema, Marmee, we've been picked to host the mother-daughter tea this year," we squealed, jumping up and down.

"Well, what an honor!" Meema said, looking at Marmee.

"That means we are going to have the tea here!" I trumpeted. "And," I looked at Meema and Marmee, "you both will have to wear long dresses with big picture hats!"

"All of the mothers will be dressed like that!" Millie added quickly.

Meema and Marmee looked at each other and shrugged. We had never seen either of them in a dress . . . ever!

"Okay," they finally said. "Well, okay."

This was going to be a first!

Meema sewed three whole nights to finish not only their dresses but Millie's and mine as well. The garden was decorated, tables rented and set. A string quartet was hired, and our mothers had the affair catered by our nonno.

After Millie and I got dressed, we waited at the bottom of the stairs for our mothers. We could hardly wait to see them.

Then they appeared at the top of the stairway. We both caught our breath.
They floated down like shimmering swans. As uncomfortable as they must have
been, they looked beautiful.

The tea was glorious. Everybody commented on how elegant everything was.
My heart still skips a beat when I think of the two of them trying so hard to
please us in those awkward, sweeping, ridiculous dresses.

How we loved them for doing this just for us.

From the day we entered our mothers' house, they prepared us for the day that we would leave it.

I was the first when I left to go away to medical school. Then Will left to study engineering. Our Millie went all the way to New York to become a fashion designer.

Of course our hearts never left our mothers' house, and over the years Will, Millie and I returned to be married in the garden, back under Thistle House.

We celebrated holidays together there. Sang at birthday parties there. Cried together when we lost our grandparents. When the three of us had our babies, all of them took their first steps in front of that clinker brick fireplace in their living room. They fell into the waiting arms of their grandmothers. Just as we had done.

We watched our mothers grow old together in that house. They passed away within a year of each other. Will, Millie and I placed them together in a green hillside overlooking the bay very near the place where they pledged their love to each other so many years ago.

Will and his family live in our mothers' house now. We were so pleased that it didn't go to a stranger, and it is still a gathering place for all of us and our families. The walls still whisper our mothers' names.

All of our hearts find peace whenever we are there . . . not only remembering them, but being there, together, in our mothers' house.

To Traci and Nikki with all of my love.

P A T R I C I A   L E E   G A U C H ,   E D I T O R

PHILOMEL BOOKS
A division of Penguin Young Readers Group.
Published by The Penguin Group.
Penguin Group (USA) Inc., 375 Hudson Street, New York, NY 10014, U.S.A.
Penguin Group (Canada), 90 Eglinton Avenue East, Suite 700, Toronto, Ontario M4P 2Y3, Canada (a division of Pearson
Penguin Canada Inc.).
Penguin Books Ltd, 80 Strand, London WC2R 0RL, England.
Penguin Ireland, 25 St. Stephen's Green, Dublin 2, Ireland (a division of Penguin Books Ltd).
Penguin Group (Australia), 250 Camberwell Road, Camberwell, Victoria 3124, Australia (a division of Pearson Australia
Group Pty Ltd).
Penguin Books India Pvt Ltd, 11 Community Centre, Panchsheel Park, New Delhi - 110 017, India.
Penguin Group (NZ), 67 Apollo Drive, Rosedale, North Shore 0632, New Zealand (a division of Pearson New Zealand Ltd).
Penguin Books (South Africa) (Pty) Ltd, 24 Sturdee Avenue, Rosebank, Johannesburg 2196, South Africa.
Penguin Books Ltd, Registered Offices: 80 Strand, London WC2R 0RL, England.

Published simultaneously in Canada.   Manufactured in China by South China Printing Co. Ltd.

Design by Semadar Megged.   Text set in 16-point Adobe Jenson.   The illustrations are rendered in pencils and markers.

Library of Congress Cataloging-in-Publication Data
Polacco, Patricia.   In our mothers' house / Patricia Polacco.   p. cm.
Summary: Three young children experience the joys and challenges of being raised by two mothers.
[1. Mothers—Fiction. 2. Family life—Fiction. 3. Lesbians—Fiction. 4. Homosexuality—Fiction.] I. Title.
PZ7.P75186Mv 2009   [E]—dc22   2008032615
ISBN 978-0-399-25076-7
5 7 9 10 8 6 4